Dear Parent:
Your child's love of reading starts here!

Every child learns to read in a different way and at his or her own speed. Some go back and forth between reading levels and read favorite books again and again. Others read through each level in order. You can help your young reader improve and become more confident by encouraging his or her own interests and abilities. From books your child reads with you to the first books he or she reads alone, there are I Can Read Books for every stage of reading:

SHARED READING
Basic language, word repetition, and whimsical illustrations, ideal for sharing with your emergent reader

BEGINNING READING
Short sentences, familiar words, and simple concepts for children eager to read on their own

READING WITH HELP
Engaging stories, longer sentences, and language play for developing readers

READING ALONE
Complex plots, challenging vocabulary, and high-interest topics for the independent reader

ADVANCED READING
Short paragraphs, chapters, and exciting themes for the perfect bridge to chapter books

I Can Read Books have introduced children to the joy of reading since 1957. Featuring award-winning authors and illustrators and a fabulous cast of beloved characters, I Can Read Books set the standard for beginning readers.

A lifetime of discovery begins with the magical words **"I Can Read!"**

*Visit www.icanread.com for information
on enriching your child's reading experience.*

For Barbara Alexandra Dicks,
who often signs her name in lower case
but is, in fact, a capital person

I Can Read Book® is a trademark of HarperCollins Publishers.

A Baby Sister for Frances. Text copyright © 1964 by Russell C. Hoban; renewed 1992 by Russell C. Hoban. Illustrations copyright © 1964, 1993 by Lillian Hoban; renewed 1992 by Lillian Hoban. Abridged edition copyright © 2011. All rights reserved. Manufactured in China. No part of this book may be used or reproduced in any manner whatsoever without written permission except in the case of brief quotations embodied in critical articles and reviews. For information address HarperCollins Children's Books, a division of HarperCollins Publishers, 10 East 53rd Street, New York, NY 10022.
www.icanread.com

Library of Congress Cataloging-in-Publication Data is available.
ISBN 978-0-06-083804-1 (trade bdg.) — ISBN 978-0-06-083806-5 (pbk.)

11 12 13 14 15   SCP   10 9 8 7 6 5 4 3 2 1   ❖   First Edition

0 1197 0673803 4

A BABY SISTER
FOR FRANCES

by Russell Hoban
Pictures by Lillian Hoban

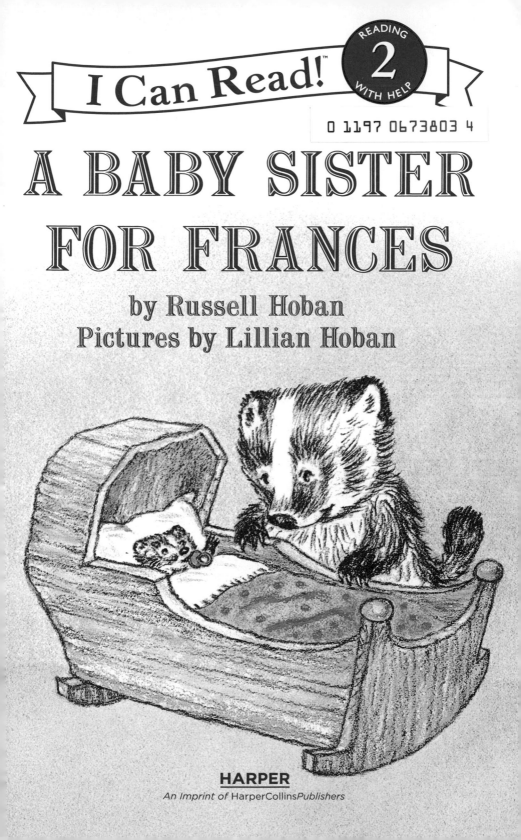

HARPER

An Imprint of HarperCollinsPublishers

It was a quiet evening.

Father was reading his newspaper.

Mother was feeding baby Gloria.

Frances was sitting under the sink.

She was singing a little song:

Plinketty, plinketty, plinketty, plink,

Here is the dishrag that's under the

sink.

Here are the buckets and brushes

and me,

Plinketty, plinketty, plinketty, plee.

She stopped the song and listened.

Nobody said anything.

Frances went into her room and took some gravel out of her drawer.

She put the gravel into a coffee can.

She marched into the living room rattling the can and singing:

Here we go marching, rattley bang!

"Please don't do that," said Father.

Frances stopped.

She went back under the sink.

Mother came in, carrying Gloria.

"Why are you sitting under the sink?" said Mother.

"It's cozy," said Frances.

"Would you like to help me put Gloria to bed?" said Mother.

"How much allowance does Gloria get?"
said Frances.

"Only big girls like you
get allowances," said Father.

"May I have a penny with my nickel
now that I am a big sister?"
said Frances.

"Yes," said Father.

"Now you will get six cents a week."

"Thank you," said Frances.

"I know a girl who gets seventeen cents.
She gets three nickels and two pennies."

"Well," said Father, "it's time for bed."

Father picked Frances up

and gave her a piggyback ride to bed.

Mother and Father tucked Frances in
and kissed her good night.
"I need my tiny special blanket,"
said Frances.
Mother gave her the special blanket.
"And I need my tricycle and my sled
and both teddy bears
and my alligator doll," said Frances.
Father brought in the tricycle
and the sled and both teddy bears
and the alligator doll.
Mother and Father kissed her good night
again and Frances went to sleep.

In the morning Frances got up and
washed and began to dress for school.
"Is my blue dress ready for me
to wear?" said Frances.
"Oh, dear," said Mother,
"I was so busy with Gloria
that I did not have time to iron it,
so you'll have to wear the yellow one."
Mother buttoned Frances up the back.
Then she brushed her hair
and put a new ribbon in it
and put her breakfast on the table.

"Why did you put sliced bananas
on the oatmeal?" said Frances.
"Did you forget that I like raisins?"
"No, I did not forget," said Mother,
"but you finished up the raisins
yesterday and I have not been out
shopping yet."

"Well," said Frances, "things are not very good around here anymore.

No clothes to wear.

No raisins for the oatmeal.

I think maybe I'll run away."

"Finish your breakfast," said Mother.

"What time will dinner be tonight?" said Frances.

"Half past six," said Mother.

"Then I will have time to run away after dinner," said Frances, and she kissed her mother good-bye and went to school.

After dinner that evening
Frances packed her little knapsack
very carefully.
She put in her tiny special blanket
and her alligator doll.
She took all of the nickels and pennies
out of her bank, for travel money,
and she took her good luck coin
for good luck.
Then she took a box of prunes
from the kitchen
and five chocolate sandwich cookies.

"Well," said Frances, "it is time
to say good-bye.
I am on my way. Good-bye."
"Where are you running away to?"
said Father.
"I think that under the dining-room
table is the best place," said Frances.
"It's cozy, and the kitchen is near
if I run out of cookies."
"That is a good place to run away to,"
said Mother, "but I'll miss you."
"I'll miss you too," said Father.

"Well," said Frances, "good-bye,"
and she ran away.

Father sat down with his newspaper.

Mother took up her knitting.

"You know, it is not the same house without Frances," said Father.

"That is *exactly* what I was thinking," said Mother.

"The place seems empty without her."

Frances sat under the dining-room table and ate her prunes.

"Even Gloria can feel it," said Mother.

"A girl looks up to a big sister."

"I can hear her crying a little right now," said Father.

Father picked up his newspaper.

Then he put it down again.

"I miss the songs that Frances

used to sing," he said.

"I was *so* fond of those little songs,"

said Mother.

"Do you remember the one

about the tomato?

'What does the tomato say,

early in the dawn?'" sang Mother.

" 'Time to be all red again,

now that night is gone,' " sang Father.

"Yes," he said, "that is a good one,

but my favorite has always been:

'When the wasps and the bumblebees

have a party, nobody comes that can't

buzz. . . .' "

"Well," said Mother, "we shall just have

to get used to a quiet house now."

29

Frances ate three sandwich cookies

and put the other two aside for later.

She began to sing:

I am poor and hungry here,

eating prunes and rice.

Living all alone is not

really very nice.

She had no rice,

but chocolate sandwich cookies

did not sound right for the song.

"I can almost hear her now," said Father,
humming the tune that Frances
had just sung.

"She has a charming voice."

"It is just not a *family* without Frances,"
said Mother.

"Babies are very nice.
Goodness knows I *like* babies,
but a baby is not a family."

"Isn't that a fact!" said Father.

"A family is *everybody all together.*"

"Think how lucky Gloria is to have
a sister like Frances," said Mother.

"I agree," said Father,
"and I hope that Gloria turns out to be
as clever and good as Frances."

"With a big sister like Frances,
she will turn out fine," said Mother.

"I'd like to hear from Frances,"
said Father, "just to know how she is."

"I'd like to hear from Frances too,"
said Mother, "and I'm not sure
the sleeves are right on this sweater
I'm knitting for her."

"Hello," called Frances

from the dining room.

"I am calling on the telephone.

Hello, hello, this is me.

Is that you?"

"Hello," said Mother.

"This is us.

How are you?"

"I am fine," said Frances.

"This is a nice place,

but you miss your family

when you're away.

How are you?"

"We are all well," said Father,

"but we miss you too."

"I will be home soon," said Frances,

and she hung up.

"Frances said that she will be home soon," said Father.

"I think I'll bake a cake," said Mother.

Frances put on her knapsack and sang a little traveling song:

Big sisters really have to stay
At home, not travel far away,
Because everybody misses them
And wants to hug-and-kisses them.

"I'm not sure about that last rhyme," said Frances as she arrived
in the living room.

"That's a good enough rhyme,"
said Father.
"I like it fine," said Mother,
and they both hugged and kissed her.

"What kind of cake are you baking?"
said Frances to Mother.

"Chocolate," said Mother.

"It's too bad that Gloria's too little
to have some," said Frances,

"but when she's a big girl like me,
she can have chocolate cake too."

"Oh, yes," said Mother,

"you may be sure that
there will always be plenty
of chocolate cake around here."

The End